DISNEP'S

THE
LION KING

Just Can't Wait to Be King

Adapted from the animated film by
Gabrielle Charbonnet

DISNEP
PRESS

New York

Contents

Chapter One

The Circle of Life

It was still dark outside, and chilly. But the young lion prince, Simba, was awake in an instant. Today was the day! Today his father, King Mufasa, was going to teach him special things—things a lion prince should know.

Simba's parents were curled up together at the back of their cozy cave. Carefully Simba stepped over the sleeping forms of the other lions in his father's pride.

"Dad?" he said, tapping his father's ear with one paw. "Dad, wake up!"

Mufasa didn't stir. Simba's mother, Sarabi,

 murmured, "Your son is awake."

"Before sunrise, he's *your* son," Mufasa grumbled sleepily.

"Come on, Dad," Simba pleaded. "You promised!"

Mufasa opened his eyes, stretched, and yawned. "Okay, okay. I'm up."

Happily Simba trotted ahead of Mufasa as they headed up to Pride Rock. The sun was just starting to tint the horizon with shades of gold and pink.

"Look, Simba," said Mufasa. "Everything the light touches is our kingdom."

"Wow," said Simba. The plains stretched away before him as far as he could see. There were fields of golden grass, and green hills, and trees and rivers.

"A king's time as ruler rises and sets like

2

the sun," said Mufasa. "One day, Simba, the sun will set on my time here. It will rise again with you as the new king."

"And all this will be mine?" Simba asked.

"Everything the light touches," Mufasa said. "Everything except that shadowy place beyond our borders. You must never go there, Simba."

"I thought a king can go wherever he wants," said Simba.

Mufasa chuckled. "There's more to being a king than doing whatever you want all the time."

Together Mufasa and Simba leaped down from Pride Rock. They headed out into the Pride Lands.

"All the animals you see belong here," Mufasa explained. "We all live together in a delicate balance. As king, you will need to respect that balance and all the creatures—from an ant to an antelope—who live here."

"But Dad, don't we eat the antelope?" asked Simba.

"Yes," Mufasa said. "But when we die, our bodies become the grass, and the antelope eat the grass. So we are all connected in the great Circle of Life."

"I see," said Simba. "Gosh." His father's job as king was much more complicated than Simba had thought.

Just then his father's advisor, Zazu, flew in with the morning report. "Good morning, Sire, young Simba. Just thought I'd check in. *Ahem.*" The hornbill cleared his throat. "The baboons are going ape, but the giraffes are acting like they're above it all. The leopards are in a bit of a spot, as usual—"

Zazu was interrupted by a mole popping up beneath him.

"Sir! News from the underground!" the mole cried. "Hyenas have been spotted in the Pride Lands!"

"Hyenas!" cried Zazu.

"Take Simba home, Zazu," Mufasa commanded.

"Can't I go with you, Dad?" Simba asked.

"No, son." Mufasa's voice was stern. Without another word, he ran off into the tall grass.

"I never get to go anywhere," Simba complained as he and Zazu turned toward home.

"Well, one day you will be king," Zazu said. "Then *you* can chase those slobbering, mangy, stupid poachers all you want."

"Yeah?" Simba cheered up. There was so much to look forward to—when he was king!

Chapter Two

The Elephant Graveyard

After Zazu brought Simba safely home, he flew off to help Mufasa. Simba trotted along, thinking over all his father had told him. On a rocky ledge not far from home, he ran into Scar, Mufasa's brother.

"Hey, Uncle Scar!" Simba cried, eager to share his news. "Guess what? I'm going to be the king of Pride Rock! My dad just showed me the whole kingdom, and I'm going to rule it someday."

"Well," said Uncle Scar, looking bored. "Isn't that special."

S i m b a
p r o u d l y
puffed out
his chest.
He didn't see
his uncle very
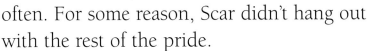
often. For some reason, Scar didn't hang out
with the rest of the pride.

"So, your father showed you the whole
kingdom, did he?" Scar asked. "Including
what's behind the northern border?"

Simba frowned. "Well, no. He said I
couldn't go there."

"And he's right!" said Scar. "An elephant
graveyard is no place for a young cub. Only
the bravest lions go there."

"I'm brave!" Simba said. "An elephant
graveyard . . . that sounds so cool."

"Oh, no," said Uncle Scar. "No matter
how brave you are—promise me you'll never
visit that awful, *dangerous*, exciting place.
Okay?"

"Okay," Simba said slowly. But in his mind, a plan was already hatching.

Back at Pride Rock, Simba found his best friend, Nala.

"Hey, Nala!" he called. "Come on! I just heard about this great place." He knew that Nala was always ready for an adventure.

"Mom, can I go with Simba?" Nala asked.

"I guess so," Nala's mother replied.

"Great!" Simba said. "Back later, Mom!"

"Hold on," Sarabi told him. "Zazu, please go with Simba and Nala."

"No, Mom!" cried Simba. Zazu would ruin everything. He knew Simba wasn't supposed to leave the Pride Lands.

"Yes, Simba," said Sarabi firmly.

So with Zazu fluttering behind them, Simba and Nala set off for the northern border.

"We've got to lose Zazu," Simba whispered to Nala. "We're going to the elephant graveyard."

"The elephant graveyard!" Nala's eyes widened. "I have an idea. Let's run into the jungle. We can lose Zazu in there."

"Good plan," said Simba.

The nearby jungle was dark and crowded with plants. As the two young cubs padded quietly on the ground, Zazu tried to keep up. But again and again he bumped into a tree, a hanging vine, the trunk of a palm. In no time at all, the cubs were able to silently slip out of sight.

"All right! It worked!" Simba shouted when they were out of Zazu's range.

"I'm brilliant, admit it," said Nala.

"Oh, yeah?" Playfully Simba leaped on Nala, and they wrestled on the ground. Nala soon pinned Simba flat.

"Hey! Let me up!" Simba laughed.

Nala released him, and they set off again. The land became less familiar and more spooky. Instead of healthy grass and trees, there were bare dirt and rocks. Everything was gray and dead-looking. Even the sky seemed to darken.

They spotted the elephant graveyard. There were bones everywhere.

"An elephant skull!" Simba said, staring.

"It's really creepy," said Nala. "We could get in so much trouble."

Simba grinned. "I know. Let's check it out."

"Hold it, young man!" snapped an irritated voice.

Simba and Nala jumped.

Zazu flapped down from his perch and glared at them accusingly. "The only checking out you do will be to check out of here. This place is very dangerous."

"Danger? Ha!" Simba said bravely. "I laugh in the face of danger." He stalked through an old elephant ribcage. "Ha-ha-ha!"

An eerie echo floated out from the tangle of bones: "Ha-ha-ha! Hee-hee-hee!"

Simba whirled to see three mangy, vicious hyenas slowly closing in on them.

Chapter Three

The Stampede

"*Well, well. Trespassers,*" *one hyena said. She looked Simba over and licked her chops.*

"Yeah," said another hyena. "Why don't you cubs stick around for . . . dinner?" He snickered meanly.

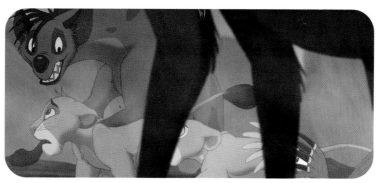

"We could have whatever's *lion* around, if you get what I'm saying," said the first hyena.

"Make mine a *cub* sandwich!" said the second one.

The third hyena just giggled.

Simba caught Nala's eye. She looked as scared as he felt. I am the future king, Simba told himself. I must not show fear.

"One, two, three," he whispered.

Nala nodded to show she understood.

"Run!" Simba shouted.

The two cubs tore off through the graveyard with the hyenas chasing after them. But Simba and Nala didn't know where they were going, and soon the hyenas had them cornered.

Simba realized that he would have to fight. He had to protect Nala. Facing the three hyenas, he drew in a deep breath and let out his fiercest roar. But he was so scared, it came out a tiny squeak.

"That was it?" laughed the first hyena. "Oh, man!"

Simba tried again. *"Rrrr-rr . . . ROAR!"*

Simba's eyes popped wide open. He knew that roar.

Huge and furious, Mufasa leaped into the clearing.

The hyenas whirled and raced off, whimpering.

Simba hung his head. He was in major trouble now.

"Zazu!" Mufasa snapped. "Take Nala home. I've got to teach my son a lesson."

Nala slunk off into the tall grass, with Zazu fluttering above her.

"I'm sorry, Dad," Simba said softly.

"You could have been killed!" said Mufasa. "Not only that, but you also put Nala in danger. I'm very disappointed in you."

Simba sniffed. He hated letting his dad down.

Mufasa put his paw around Simba's shoulders. "Look, son. Being brave doesn't mean you go looking for trouble. I was so afraid today . . . when I thought I might lose you."

"You won't ever lose me, Dad," Simba said. "We'll be together forever, right?"

"Simba, look at the stars," said Mufasa.

Night had fallen during the hyenas' wild chase. Above, twinkling silver lights dotted the dark sky.

"The great kings of the past look down on us from those stars," Mufasa continued.

"Whenever you feel alone, remember that those kings will always be there to guide you. And so will I."

Simba leaned against his father, taking comfort in his strength. There was so much Mufasa had to teach him.

A few days later, Simba's Uncle Scar came to find him.

"Your father sent me to get you," said Scar.

Ever since the hyena incident, Simba had been on his best behavior. So he trotted quickly alongside Scar as they headed for a deep gorge. If Mufasa needed him, he would be there.

At the very bottom of the gorge was a small tree with a rock below it. Scar led Simba to it.

"Wait here," Scar said. "Your father has a wonderful surprise for you."

"Oh, boy," said Simba. "Will I like the surprise?"

"Simba—it's to die for," said Scar. He turned and loped off, leaving Simba alone.

Simba grew bored waiting for his father. But he knew better than to disobey Mufasa again. While he waited on the rock, he decided to practice his roar. It was getting better all the time.

A few minutes later Simba noticed that the ground was trembling. Then he heard a dim, far-off rumble. He looked around the gorge. Way at the far end, a swarm of dark forms poured down the ledge. Simba squinted. As the cloud grew closer, Simba saw it was wildebeests—hundreds and thousands of wildebeests. They were stampeding!

Quickly Simba climbed to the top of the small tree. He gulped, his eyes wide with fear. Wildebeests were large and heavy, and they had sharp horns. With this many of them stampeding, they were unstoppable. There was no escape—Simba was going to be trampled!

Chapter Four

The Rescue

Simba clung to his branch, his claws digging into its rough bark. The whole world was shaking. Simba's teeth rattled in his head, and his branch started dipping toward the stream of shaggy animals rushing beneath him. His grip was slipping.

"Simba! Hold on!" Zazu flapped overhead, choking on the dust. "Your father is on his way!"

At that moment a wildebeest ran smack into the tree, knocking Simba right off his branch.

"Aaaaaah!" he screamed. With a *thunk* Simba fell into his father's solid paws. Mufasa was here!

Grabbing Simba in his powerful jaws, Mufasa leaped out of the stampede's path and sprang up a rocky ledge. He put Simba down.

Simba took a deep breath of relief.

But it was too soon to relax. A large wildebeest knocked into the ledge, and Mufasa lost his footing. The king slipped over the side.

"Dad!" Simba cried. "Dad!"

Creeping close to the edge, Simba peered down. Where was Mufasa? What was happening? Then Mufasa appeared on a lower ledge. As Simba watched in horror, his father slowly slid down the side and disappeared into the surging stampede.

"Noooo!" Simba screamed.

It seemed like forever before the stampede was over. The wildebeests thundered out the other end of the gorge. Behind them, nothing but flattened plants, clouds of dust, rubble, and . . . Mufasa.

Clumsily Simba climbed down from his ledge. He ran to where his father lay, silent and still, on the trampled gorge floor.

"Dad?" Simba said softly. He touched his father's face with one paw. "Please, Dad, wake up. You can wake up—it's safe now."

But Mufasa didn't move.

Simba started to panic. "Help!" he cried. "Please, somebody, help!"

Simba scanned the skies for Zazu, for anyone. But there was no one. And somehow, Simba knew that his father would never rise again.

"Simba." A deep voice made Simba turn around.

"Uncle Scar!" Simba sobbed. "There were wildebeests. . . . Dad saved me. . . . It was an accident. I didn't know—"

"No, of *course* you didn't," said his uncle. "But now the king is dead. If it weren't for

you, he'd still be alive. What is your mother going to think?"

Simba stared at Scar, horrified. In just one morning, his whole world had collapsed. "What am I going to do?" he asked.

"Run away, Simba," Scar said, his lip curling. "If you go home, everyone will know that you killed your own father, the king. So run away and never return."

Shocked, Simba stared at his uncle. Uncle Scar must be right. He must know the best thing to do, Simba thought. Without even saying good-bye, Simba turned and ran toward the end of the gorge. He ran and ran, as fast as he could possibly go.

Chapter Five

New Friends

How long he ran, Simba didn't know. When he was too tired to run, he trotted. When he couldn't trot any more, he walked. And so on he went, till the grassy plain gave way to hard-baked earth. Till everything familiar was gone. Till there was nothing around him but scorched land, shimmering sun, and endless, white-hot sky.

He was thirsty. He was more than thirsty. Hot dust choked him and caked his nose. He felt dizzy and sick and more tired than he had ever been in his life.

Finally he simply couldn't go on. Had he come far enough? He didn't know. But he had gone as far as he could. Without caring, Simba collapsed on the ground and closed his eyes.

Splash. A trickle of cold water running down his ear made Simba open his eyes. *Splash.* He blinked groggily. Was it raining? He blinked again.

"You okay, kid?" said a voice.

Simba looked up to see a small meerkat smiling down at him.

"I . . . guess so," Simba said, feeling as if he would never be okay again.

"You nearly died," said a large warthog nearby.

"I saved you," said the meerkat. "I'm Timon. This is Pumbaa. He helped save you, a little bit."

Simba staggered to his feet. His paws felt burned and raw. He was starving and very tired. But he knew he had to leave.

"Thanks for your help," he said quietly as he walked away.

"Hey, where are you going?" Timon called.

"Nowhere," Simba answered forlornly.

Timon and Pumbaa ran after him. "Wait!" said Timon. "What's your name? Where are you from? What's wrong?"

"My name is Simba. It doesn't matter where I'm from because I can never go back. I . . . I did something terrible. But I don't want to talk about it."

"Good!" said Timon cheerfully. "Because we don't want to hear about it."

"Yeah!" said Pumbaa. "You've got to put your behind in your past."

Timon shook his head. "No, no, no! He means, you've got to put your *past* behind you. Look, kid. Sometimes bad things happen, and you can't do anything about it, right?"

Simba looked at him. "Right." That was just how he felt about his father's death.

"Wrong!" said Timon. "I always say, when the world turns its back on you, you turn your back on the world."

"That's not what I was taught," said Simba.

"Then maybe you need a new lesson," Timon said. "Repeat after me: *hakuna matata*."

Simba frowned. "Haku—what?"

"Ha-ku-na ma-ta-ta," said Pumbaa slowly. "It means 'no worries.' It's our motto. Those two words will solve all your problems."

"No worries?" Simba asked.

"That's right!" said Timon. "It means leave the past alone. It's over. Live in the present.

That's where it's all happening. Right, Pumbaa?"

"Right!" rumbled the warthog. "Hakuna matata."

Hakuna matata sounded awfully tempting to Simba. Everything about his past—his mother, his father, even Nala—just hurt to think about. He had to accept the fact that they were gone . . . forever. Somehow, he must keep living. Now he had two new friends willing to help him. They didn't care about his past. He could start all over, here, far from home.

Simba looked at Timon and Pumbaa. "Hakuna matata," he said.

Chapter Six

Hakuna Matata

It wasn't far from the sunbaked plain where Simba had almost died to the lush, green jungle Simba's new friends called home.

"It's beautiful here," Simba said. For just a moment he thought about Pride Rock, about the golden, grassy plains where his father had been king. Then he shook his head. Those days were over now.

"Gee, I'm starved," Pumbaa said, breaking into Simba's thoughts.

"Me too," said Simba. "I could eat a whole zebra!"

Timon looked uncomfortable. "Uh, we're fresh out of zebra."

"Any antelope? Hippo?" Simba asked hopefully.

"No, and no," said Timon. "Listen, kid, if you live with us, you have to eat like us." He stepped forward and pushed over a rotten log. "Hey, now this looks like a good spot to rustle up some grub." He picked up a thick, wiggly worm and held it out.

Simba wrinkled his nose. "Ew. What's that?"

"A grub," said Timon. "Yum!" He popped it into his mouth and chewed. "Tastes like chicken."

Pumbaa slurped down a grub, too. "Slimy, yet satisfying."

Simba gazed at his new friends. He'd really like a nice antelope sandwich, with maybe some little groundhogs on the side. But he lived here now. Timon was right. He would have to eat like them.

Timon held out a shiny green leaf covered with wiggling things. "Try this one," he said, pointing. "They're crunchy on the outside, chewy on the inside."

"Oh, well," Simba said. "Hakuna matata." He picked up a plump grub and ate it. "Not bad," he said in surprise. "Slimy, yet satisfying."

"That's the way, kid," said Pumbaa. "Now you're one of us."

From that day on, Simba refused to think about the past. With Timon and Pumbaa, he lived each day as it came. He woke up when he wanted, slept when he wanted, ate when he wanted.

Almost without realizing it, Simba grew bigger and stronger. His mane became thick and dark. His muscles filled out and his coat lost its cubby softness.

One day he looked at his reflection in the river and saw a grown-up lion looking back at him. He was still the same Simba underneath, but on the outside he looked different. He looked like Mufasa, and that made him sad.

That evening the three friends gorged themselves on a whole mound of termites

they had found. Afterward they lay on their backs on a grassy hill and gazed at the stars.

"Whoa, am I stuffed," said Pumbaa. "I ate like a pig."

"Pumbaa," Simba reminded him. "You *are* a pig."

"Oh, right." Pumbaa burped. "Hey, you guys. Ever wonder what those sparkly dots up there are?"

"They're fireflies," said Timon matter-of-factly. "Fireflies that got stuck up on that big bluish-black thing."

"Oh, gee," said Pumbaa. "I always thought they were huge balls of gas, burning billions of miles away."

"Pumbaa," said Timon. "With you, *every-thing's* gas."

"Somebody once told me that the great kings of the past are up there, watching over us," Simba said softly.

"You mean a bunch of royal dead guys are watching us?" said Timon. "Who told you something like that?" He slapped his knees and laughed. "What dummy made that up?"

Pumbaa was chuckling.

Simba forced himself to laugh a little. "Yeah, pretty dumb, huh?" he said.

"Hysterical!" Timon said.

Feeling a deep sadness he couldn't explain, Simba got up and wandered off. He needed time to think. All of a sudden, something seemed to be missing from his life. But what?

Chapter Seven

Nala

After being with Timon and Pumbaa so long, Simba had nearly forgotten that most lions didn't live the way he did: eating grubs and having friends better suited for a meal.

He was used to it, but any other lion would—

"Hellllp!" Pumbaa shrieked.

In seconds Simba had raced to where his friend was shouting in terror.

Springing into the clearing, Simba saw a female lion stalking Pumbaa, trapped under a fallen tree. Timon was struggling to free his

friend. The lioness was slinking closer, tail lashing, fangs showing.

"*ROAR!*" Even Simba was surprised by how loud and fierce his own voice had become. He leaped toward the lioness, but she was ready for him. Together they rolled across the ground, snarling and fighting.

Suddenly Simba found himself pinned to the ground with the lioness hanging over him. It was familiar somehow. . . . *She* was familiar. But who . . . ?

"Nala?" Simba asked, his eyes widening.

The lioness drew back, shocked.

"Is it you?" Simba asked with a rush of joy. His childhood friend he'd thought he'd never see again!

"Who are you?" she asked suspiciously.

"It's me, Simba," he answered.

She frowned at him.

"It's really me, Nala. Believe me."

The distrust on her face changed to amazement and happiness. "Simba! But how did you—where did you come from?"

"It's so good to see you," said Simba. "What are you doing here?" He circled her happily. Like him, she had grown big and strong.

"I asked first," said Nala. "What are *you* doing here?"

"Hey," said Timon. "Excuse me, but WHAT IS GOING ON HERE?"

Simba had forgotten all about Timon and Pumbaa! "Timon, this is Nala," he explained. "She's my best friend."

Pumbaa squeezed out from under the tree.

"Nala, this is Pumbaa," said Simba. "Pumbaa, Nala."

"Pleased to meet you," Pumbaa said cheerfully.

"The pleasure's all mine," said Nala.

"Wait a minute," Timon snapped. "Let me

get this straight. You guys know each other. But she wants to *eat* Pumbaa. And everybody's okay with this?"

Simba laughed. "Relax, Timon."

"Wait till everyone finds out you've been here all this time," Nala said excitedly. "Your mother will be so happy!"

Painful memories flooded back. "She doesn't have to know," Simba said quickly. "No one has to know."

"Of course they do!" Nala said. "Everyone thinks you're dead. Scar told us about the stampede."

"And . . . what else did he tell you?" Simba asked.

"What else matters?" Nala exclaimed. "You're alive! And that means . . . you're the king." She looked awed.

Timon burst out laughing. "Oh, right! He's the king!" He slapped his knees and shook his head. "The king! Him! That is too funny."

"He truly is the rightful king," Nala insisted.

"Your Majesty," Pumbaa said, bowing.

"Oh, stop it," Simba muttered.

"Pumbaa," said Timon. "Don't be silly. He's not the king. Are you?" he asked Simba.

"No," Simba said. "I mean—maybe I was going to be. But that was a long time ago."

Timon's jaw dropped open. "You mean— you're the king? You've been the king all this time and you never told us?"

"Look, I'm still the same guy," Simba said.

"Oh, Simba," said Nala. "You don't know what this will mean to everyone. Things at home—they're terrible. Scar is king—and he let the hyenas take over the Pride Lands."

"What?" Simba was shocked. He had tried not to think of home. Now he realized that things he'd never imagined had happened to those he loved.

"Everything's destroyed," Nala continued sadly. "There's no food, no water. Simba—if you don't help us, we'll starve."

"But . . . I can't go back," Simba said.

Chapter Eight

Simba Remembers

Nala stared at him. "What do you mean? You have to do something."

"No, I don't," said Simba. "I don't have to go home. I don't have to do anything. Nothing matters. Hakuna matata."

"What does that mean?" Nala asked.

"It means sometimes bad things happen, and there's nothing you can do about it. So why worry?" He started to walk away.

"It's your responsibility!" Nala cried, running after him.

"But *you* left," Simba pointed out.

"I left to find help!" said Nala. "And I found you. Don't you understand? You're our only hope."

"Sorry." Simba tried not to see how hurt Nala was.

"You really disappoint me," said Nala.

"You know, you're starting to sound like my father," Simba said angrily.

"Good!" Nala replied just as angrily. "At least someone does."

"Look, just forget it," Simba snapped. "You don't know anything. Just leave me alone."

"Fine!" Nala shouted. "I will!"

This time when Simba turned to go, she didn't follow him.

That evening Simba stalked off into the jungle. He was upset and confused and angry. For once, hakuna matata didn't seem to be solving his problems.

The black sky loomed overhead. Simba gazed at the twinkling stars. "Dad, you said you'd always be there for me. But you're not," Simba said. "And it's because of me. It's all my fault."

Simba dropped down beneath a tree and rested his head on his paws. He was sorry he had argued with Nala. But she was wrong about him—he wasn't a hero. He couldn't help.

Thunk! A pebble hit Simba's head. He glared up at an old baboon who was sitting in the tree.

"Hey! Knock it off!" Simba said.

The baboon grinned at him.

Frowning, Simba got up and walked off.

The baboon jumped down and came after him, singing a nonsense song.

"Quit following me," Simba commanded. "Creepy little monkey. Who are you, anyway?"

"Rafiki," said the baboon. "The question is, who are you?"

Simba sighed. "I thought I knew once. Now I'm not sure."

Rafiki laughed. "Well, I know who you are. You're Mufasa's boy. Bye!" He turned and ran.

Simba stared after him in shock, then followed him. "Hey! Wait!" he called. "You knew my father?"

The baboon ran faster than Simba expected. It was some time before Simba caught up with him.

"Correction," said Rafiki. "I *know* your father."

"I hate to tell you this," said Simba. "But my father died a long time ago."

"Wrong," said Rafiki. "Mufasa is alive. I'll show you."

He led Simba to the edge of a pond. But when Simba looked into the water, he saw only his own reflection.

"That's just me," Simba said in disappointment.

"Look harder," said Rafiki.

Slowly the reflection changed to show Mufasa's face. Simba gasped.

"You see, he lives in you," Rafiki said.

"Simba, you have forgotten me," said Mufasa's voice.

"No! Dad—," Simba said.

"Look inside yourself, Simba," Mufasa said. "You are more than what you have become. You must take your place in the Circle of Life."

"How can I?" Simba cried.

"Remember who you are," said his father. "You are my son, and the one true king. Remember who you are. . . ."

"Dad! Wait!" Simba said, but the reflection was already fading. "Please don't leave me—again."

When Mufasa was gone, Rafiki sat down beside Simba.

"The past can hurt," said Rafiki. "But you cannot run away from it. You must learn from the pain you feel."

"It's not that easy," Simba said. "Going back after running away for so long . . ."

"You can do it," Rafiki said. "You can do it—because you are Mufasa's son."

Suddenly Simba knew Rafiki was right. He could no longer run away from the truth. And the truth was: Simba was king. And he had to help his kingdom. He headed for home.

Chapter Nine

King Simba

The distance that had seemed to take forever when Simba was just a little cub now was surprisingly short. Soon he was at the very edge of the Pride Lands. At least, he thought they were the Pride Lands. But the lush, grassy plains were now bare sun-dried dirt. Acacia trees were stripped of their leaves and stood withered and bent. The river and its watering hole were just dusty ridges in the ground.

"Simba!" Nala ran up behind him, panting. "I had to follow you. It's awful, isn't it?"

"I didn't want to believe you," said Simba. "But I realized I had to come back. After all, this is my kingdom. If I don't fight for it, who will?"

"I will," Nala said.

Simba smiled at her. "It will be dangerous," he warned.

"Danger? Ha!" Nala grinned. "I laugh in the face of danger."

They shared that happy memory together, then Simba squinted as a slow cloud of dust approached them.

"Timon! Pumbaa!" he said.

Pumbaa snorted and shook the dust off. "At your service, Your Highness."

Timon looked at the ruined lands. "We're going to fight your uncle for *this*?" he asked. "Talk about your fixer-upper! But if it's important to you . . . we're with you to the end."

Simba gave his friends a grateful hug. Then they all set off for Pride Rock.

Their plan was simple: while Timon and Pumbaa distracted the hyenas, Nala would rally the other lionesses. Simba himself would tackle Scar.

"Hey! Dog-boy! Over here!" Timon shouted. A group of mangy hyenas looked up. When they saw the meerkat and the juicy warthog, they licked their lips.

"How about a nice ham sandwich?" Timon yelled, pointing at Pumbaa. Then he and Pumbaa turned and raced out of there as fast as they could. The hyenas, howling and slobbering, tore off after them.

With the path clear, Simba leaped up to the pride's cave near the top of Pride Rock. Everything looked so much smaller now—because he was so much bigger.

Just outside the cave, his Uncle Scar was arguing with Sarabi, Simba's mother. Simba stayed hidden for a moment.

"It's over, Scar," Sarabi was saying. "There's no food or water. We must leave Pride Rock."

"No!" Scar snapped. "I am king, and I say we stay here. You'll just have to look harder for food."

"If you were half the king Mufasa was—," Sarabi began.

"Don't you dare mention that name to me!" Scar roared, and he cuffed Sarabi hard with his open paw. Simba snarled as he saw his mother fall.

"*ROAR!*" With a mighty battle cry, Simba lunged toward Scar.

"Mufasa?" Scar said, afraid. "No. You're dead. It can't be."

"It's Simba. I've come home," growled Simba. "Give me one good reason why I shouldn't rip you apart."

"Maybe because all the *hyenas* think I'm the king," said Scar smoothly.

"But *we* all think Simba's king," called Nala.

Simba looked around to see Nala surrounded by the pride's lionesses, all nodding in agreement.

"The choice is yours, Scar," said Simba. "Step down, or fight."

"Are you sure they want you as king? Maybe they don't know who was responsible for Mufasa's death," said Scar.

Simba took a deep, painful breath. Here was his past. Only if he faced it would he be able to face the future.

"I am," Simba said clearly.

"Simba!" Sarabi cried.

"It's true, Mother," Simba said gently. "It's my fault Dad died. But it was an accident."

"But this isn't!" shouted Scar, leaping at Simba.

Caught unaware, Simba was shoved over the ledge. But he grabbed onto its edge with his front claws.

Scar leaned over him. "I don't think they'll buy the accident part, Simba," he said in a low

snarl. "Thank goodness they don't know that *I* killed Mufasa because I wanted to be king."

All at once everything made sense: this had been Scar's plan all along. He'd wanted to get rid of both Mufasa and Simba so that *he* could rule the pride. A new, fierce anger burned in Simba. All those years he had lived in exile—and it wasn't his fault that Mufasa had died. None of it was his fault.

With the anger came a new strength. Roaring mightily he leaped back onto the rock and faced Scar. "Murderer!" he shouted, pushing Scar toward the cliff.

"Tell them," Simba said, raising one paw. "Loudly, so they can hear you."

Scar looked down. Simba made a motion to push him over the edge. "Okay! Okay! I did it," Scar said. "I killed Mufasa."

The lionesses leaped forward, just as Scar's army of hyenas returned. The battle for Pride Rock began as a bolt of lightning struck, setting the land ablaze.

Scar was used to having others fight for him. It wasn't long before Simba overpowered him, high on Pride Rock.

"It was all the hyenas' fault," Scar whined. "It was their idea. They're the enemy."

"You're lying," Simba said. "Everything you've ever told me is a lie."

"I'll make it up to you, Simba," Scar said. "Ask for anything you want. I'll do anything."

"Then run away," Simba growled. "Run away and never come back."

"Certainly, Your Majesty," Scar said, bending low. But suddenly he scooped up a pawful of coals and flung it in Simba's face.

Simba leaped for him, and they rolled, fighting toward the edge.

Simba got the upper hand. He threw Scar, who went over the side, screaming. Scar landed at the bottom of the cliff. Still alive, he opened his eyes and found himself face-to-face with the hyenas.

The hyenas closed in, and Scar disappeared.

A crack of thunder boomed in the distance. As Simba stood on the cliff, rain began to fall. Rafiki approached Simba and hugged him.

"It is time," he told Simba, "to take your place in the Circle of Life."

Slowly, alone, Simba climbed to the top of Pride Rock. There he stood, as king, just as Mufasa had once stood. Now King Simba threw back his head and roared.